That's Why!

For Lady Sarah Maclean

That's Why!

Babette Cole

Red Fox

Bad news in
the papers.

War
on TV.

Kids looting

and
hassling
on the
streets.

Ziggi shut it out
with his music.

He didn't see the point of anything.
"Why ever was I born?" he sighed.
"We could write a song
about that," said Albert.

The stars still twinkled over the city at night –

Ziggi and Albert sang their sad song to them.

They were lucky!
One of them was listening . . .
and was heading
their way!

The star burst!
It wasn't really a star at all.
It was an all-flying,
all-singing little stallion.

"Hold on tight," sang the little stallion.
"I'm taking you on the flight of your life.
That'll change your tune!"

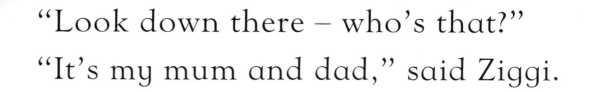

"Look down there – who's that?"
"It's my mum and dad," said Ziggi.

"They were born
to give you life,"
said the stallion.

"Doctors, nurses, dentists – they were born to keep you healthy."

"Teachers were born to help make your dreams come true. Sometimes they seem a pain, but listen to what they say.

"Your hero Deezee Jones did.

He was born to be
your inspiration."

"You'll be as good as him one day, you know."

"And here's lovely Bella. You were born
to love one another . . . and the vicar was
born to make you man and wife!"

"Here are all the kids you'll have.
They were born to be your future."

"We all have a purpose. We fit together like a jigsaw puzzle, to help one another."

"No matter who we are or where we come from, we were all born to work together. It's like music – lots of notes make one perfect tune!

Caring and sharing make
the world go round."

"But why was *I* born?" asked Ziggi. "What is *my* purpose?"
"Why, to tell everyone what you've seen,
of course!" said the little stallion.

"Sing your new song to the whole world, Ziggi."

"That's why we were born!"
"That's why!"
"That's why!"

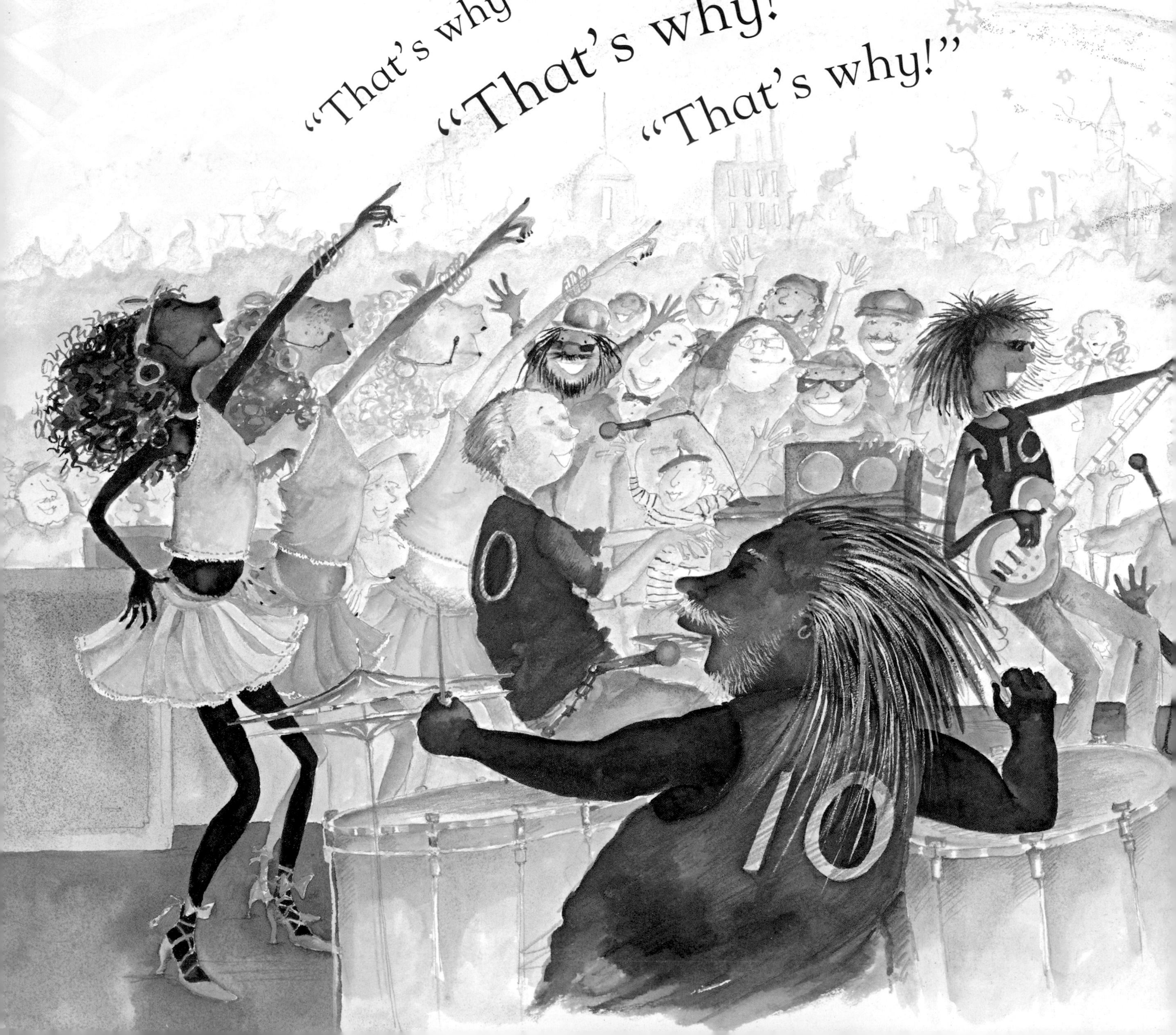

"The purpose of life is that life has
a purpose. Let's all work together
to make it better for us.
Love one another, care for each other,
that's why we were born!"

"That's why!"

That's why we were born!

THAT'S WHY
A RED FOX BOOK 978 0 099 46399 3

First published in Great Britain by Jonathan Cape,
an imprint of Random House Children's Books

Jonathan Cape edition published 2006
Red Fox edition published 2007

1 3 5 7 9 10 8 6 4 2

Red Fox Books are published by Random House Children's Books,
61–63 Uxbridge Road, London W5 5SA

www.**kidsatrandomhouse**.co.uk
www.**rbooks**.co.uk

Addresses for companies within The Random House Group Limited
can be found at: www.randomhouse.co.uk/offices.htm

THE RANDOM HOUSE GROUP Limited Reg. No. 954009

A CIP catalogue record for this book is available
from the British Library

Printed in Singapore